Once There Was and Was Not

Once There Was and Was Not

ARMENIAN TALES RETOLD

by Virginia A. Tashjian

Based on Stories by H. Toumanian

Illustrated by Nonny Hogrogian

Little, Brown and Company · *Boston* · *Toronto*

IN MEMORY OF MY SISTER ARMANE A. MANUELIAN
—AND FOR HER THREE S's—
SHANT, SHAHAN AND SEVAN

Contents

AUTHOR'S NOTE ix

THE FOOLISH MAN 3

THE MILLER-KING 13

THE MASTER AND THE SERVANT 29

THE TALKING FISH 41

SHROVETIDE 51

THE WHITE SNAKE 57

NAZAR THE BRAVE 71

Author's Note

THE ARMENIANS, *an ancient people who have lived since prehistoric times in the northeastern part of Asia Minor on a lofty plateau south of the Caucasus Mountains, have long possessed a body of folklore and legend, hero tales and tales of gods and giants almost unknown to the English-speaking world.*

Some of these tales are stories of the common folk who have the universal faults and foibles of ordinary people and who are sometimes the victims of trickery and of enchantment, while others deal with the realm of spirits and monsters.

Armenian writers and historians throughout the centuries have recorded the "other world" beings, and there have been, in the past, several writers of Armenian fables (including Mkhitar Gosh, Vartan Aiketzi, Moses Kashankatvatzi) whose stories are even today household favorites.

The seven folk tales in this collection tell of the common folk—their own quiet humor and their peculiar resolutions of problems. They are a modern retelling of stories told by folklorist Hovhannes Toumanian, who lived from 1869 to 1923.

Some of them will be reminders of folk tales from other parts of the world. A talking fish is, indeed, a well-known device used throughout folklore, while "The Miller-King" is certainly a variant of "Mighty Mikko" in Finnish folklore and of "The Good Man and the Kind Mouse" from the folklore of Chile.

Once There Was and Was Not

The Foolish Man

ONCE THERE WAS AND WAS NOT IN ANCIENT ARMENIA a poor man who worked and toiled hard from morn till night, but nevertheless remained poor.

Finally one day he became so discouraged that he decided to go in search of God in order to ask Him how long he must endure such poverty—and to beg of Him a favor.

On his way, the man met a wolf.

"Good day, brother man," asked the wolf. "Where are you bound in such a hurry?"

"I go in search of God," replied the man. "I have a complaint to lodge with him."

"Well," said the wolf, "would you do me a kindness? When you find God, will you complain to Him for me, too? Tell Him you met a half-starved wolf who searches the woods and fields for food from morning till night—and though he works hard and long, still finds nothing to eat. Ask God why He does not provide for wolves since He created them?"

"I will tell Him of your complaint," agreed the poor man, and continued on his way.

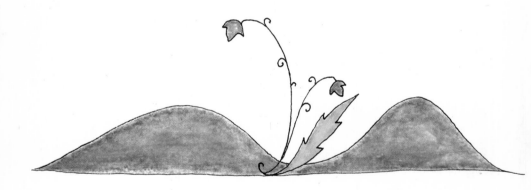

As he hurried over the hills and through the valleys, he chanced to meet a beautiful maid.

"Where do you go in such a hurry, my brother?" asked the maid.

"I go in search of God," replied the man.

4

"Oh, kind friend, when you find God, would you ask Him something for me? Tell him you met a maid on your way. Tell Him she is young and fair and very rich—but very unhappy. Ask God why she cannot know happiness. What will become of her? Ask God why He will not help her to be happy."

"I will tell Him of your trouble," promised the poor man, and continued on his way.

Soon he met a tree which seemed all dried up and dying even though it grew by the side of a river.

"Where do you go in such a hurry, O traveler?" called the dry tree.

"I go in search of God," answered the man. "I have a complaint to lodge with Him."

"Wait a moment, O traveler," begged the tree, "I, too, have a question for God.

"Please ask Him why I am dry both in summer and winter. Though I live by this wet river, my leaves do not turn green. Ask God how long I must suffer. Ask Him that for me, good friend," said the tree.

The man listened to the tree's complaint, promised to tell God, and continued once again upon his way.

Finally, the poor man reached the end of his journey. He found God seated beneath the ledge of a cliff.

"Good day," said the man as he approached God.

"Welcome, traveler," God returned his greeting. "Why have you journeyed so far? What is your trouble?"

"Well, I want to know why there is injustice in the world. Is it fair that I toil and labor from morn till night— and yet never seem to earn enough for a full stomach, while many who do not work half as hard as I live and eat as rich men do?"

"Go then," replied God. "I present you the Gift of Luck. Go find it and enjoy it to the end of your days."

"I have yet another complaint, my Lord," continued the man—and he proceeded to list the complaints and requests of the starved wolf, the beautiful maid, and the parched tree.

God gave appropriate answers to each of the three complaints, whereupon the poor man thanked Him and started on his way homeward.

Soon he came upon the dry, parched tree.

"What message did God have for me?" asked the tree.

"He said that beneath your trunk there lies a pot of gold which prevents the water from seeping up your trunk to your leaves. God said your branches will never turn green until the pot of gold is removed."

"Well, what are you waiting for, foolish man!" exclaimed the tree. "Dig up that pot of gold. It will make you rich—and permit me to turn green and live again!"

"Oh, no," protested the man. "I have no time to dig up a pot of gold. God has given me the Gift of Luck. I must hurry and search for it." And he hurried on his way.

Presently, he met the beautiful maid who was waiting for him. "Oh, kind friend, what message did God have for me?"

"God said that you will soon meet a kind man who will prove to be a good life's companion to you. No longer will you be lonely. Happiness and contentment will come to you," reported the poor man.

"In that case, what are you waiting for, foolish man?" exclaimed the maid. "Why don't you stay here and be my life's companion."

"Oh, no! I have no time to stay with you. God has given me the Gift of Luck. I must hurry and search for it." And the man hurried on his way.

Some distance away, the starving wolf impatiently awaited the man's coming, and hailed him with a shout.

"Well, what did God say? What message did He send to me?"

"Brother wolf, so many things have happened since I saw you last," said the man. "I hardly know where to begin. On my way to seek God, I met a beautiful maid who begged me to ask God the reason for her unhappiness. And I met a parched tree who wanted God to explain the dryness of its branches even though it stood by a wet river.

"I told God about these matters. He bade me tell the maid to seek a life's companion in order to find happiness. He bade me warn the tree about a pot of gold buried near its trunk which must be removed before the branches can receive nourishment from the earth.

"On my return, I brought God's answers to the maid and to the tree. The maid asked me to stay and be her life's companion, while the tree asked me to dig up the pot of gold.

"Of course, I had to refuse both since God gave me the Gift of Luck—and I must hurry along to search for it!"

"Ah-h-h, brother man, and what was God's reply to me?" asked the starving wolf.

"As for you," replied the man, "God said that you would remain hungry until you met a silly and foolish man whom you could eat up. Only then, said God, would your hunger be satisfied."

"Hmmmmmm," mused the wolf, "where in the world will I find a man more silly and stupid than you?"

And he ate up the foolish man.

The Miller-King

ONCE THERE WAS AND WAS NOT IN ANCIENT ARMENIA
a poor miller who was barely able to make ends meet. One
morning he went out to start up the waterwheel of his mill
and, when he returned, the piece of cheese he had left on
the table for his noonday meal had disappeared.

At the end of the day, he went out to shut off the waterwheel, and when he returned this time, the piece of crusty
bread he had saved for his supper had disappeared.

"How could this be?" wondered the miller. "Who is
stealing my bit of food?" And that night, he set a trap. 13

The night passed. When morning came, the miller found a fox caught fast in the trap.

"Ho! You miserable thief you! I'll show you what it is to steal my food!" shouted the miller and went after the fox with a broom.

The fox begged for mercy. "Don't kill me," he pleaded. "What is a piece of cheese or a crust of bread that you wish to kill me for that? Set me free . . . I promise to reward you for your kindness."

The miller listened and, being a kindly man at heart, set the fox free. At once, the fox hurried to the royal stable belonging to the king of that land. Searching carefully, he found a gold piece on the stable floor. Quickly he presented himself at the palace and was ushered in to the king.

"LONG LIVE YOUR MAJESTY," said the fox, bowing low. "I have come to ask a favor. My master, the miller-king who lives not far from here, is engaged in counting his gold, but alas, he has no proper means of measure. Would you kindly lend us your measuring basket? I promise you we will return it promptly."

"I have never heard of this miller-king," frowned the king. "Who is he?"

"To be sure, you do not know him yet, Your Majesty," replied the fox. "He is a very rich king, and I am his vizier.

Please lend us this measuring basket to measure his gold and then you shall meet him."

The king agreed. Taking the basket out of sight of the palace, the fox carefully placed the gold piece which he had found in the stable in the bottom of the basket. Later that evening he returned the basket to the king.

"Oh-h-h," he said, pretending to be weary, "how my master thanks you. We're both so tired, but thanks to your basket, we finally finished measuring the gold."

The king rubbed his chin. "Can it really be that this miller-king is so rich he measures his gold by the basket?" he wondered. Taking the basket, he shook it. A gold piece fell out.

The next day, the fox appeared once again before the king.

"LONG LIVE YOUR MAJESTY," he said, bowing low. "My master, the miller-king, has some precious jewels he needs to count. May we impose on Your Majesty's kindness and borrow the measuring basket once more? I promise to return it by nightfall."

Once again, the fox took the basket out of sight of the palace. He had found a pearl somewhere behind the king's stable, and he placed it in the bottom of the basket.

When evening came, he returned the basket to the king.

"Oh-h-h," he groaned, "how tired I am! We had such a time measuring all the jewels. My master deeply thanks Your Majesty for the use of the basket."

The king reached for the basket. As he did so, the pearl fell out. The amazed king wondered how anyone could be rich enough to measure precious jewels by the basket.

Several days passed. Then the fox reappeared at the palace, and this time asked the king for the hand of his daughter, the princess, as wife to the miller-king.

Remembering the riches of his neighbor, the king happily agreed to the match and ordered the palace staff to prepare at once for a wedding. All was confusion in the palace as the hasty plans got under way.

Meanwhile, the fox hurried to the flour mill and congratulated the poor miller. "I have received the king's own permission for you to have his daughter as your wife," he said. "Come! Hurry and make ready! We are going to your wedding."

"What!" exclaimed the bewildered miller. "Have you gone out of your mind? What have you done? Who am I to marry a king's daughter? I have no decent means of livelihood, no house, and not even any clothes other than the wretched things I now wear!"

"Don't worry. Leave everything to me." The fox assured the miller, and he hurried back to the king.

"Your Majesty, the most terrible tragedy has taken place," he announced. "The miller-king and his retinue were on their way here for the wedding when suddenly enemy soldiers attacked and robbed him of everything.

"Fortunately, my master escaped. He was able to take refuge in a broken-down mill not far from here. But you must give me clothes and horses so that he may come to his wedding in proper style. Then he plans to hurry on to take revenge on the enemy who attacked him."

The king immediately gave the fox some clothes fit for royalty and dispatched enough horses and guards to escort his future son-in-law properly to his bride's home.

The fox hurried back to the mill with the clothes. Long before the guards and horses arrived he had dressed the poor miller in the princely garments. Then he helped him mount one of the royal horses.

Escorted by the palace guards, the miller arrived at the palace in a solemn, dignified procession. The poor miller, who had never seen a palace before in his life, was tongue-tied. He looked about him in amazement. He stared first at his own clothes, then at the finery about him, and was unable to utter a word.

"Why does your master stare about so, brother fox?" asked the king. "You would almost think he had never seen such clothes or even such a palace."

"Oh, no, Your Majesty, it isn't that at all! He is simply comparing your palace with his own. Of course, he finds quite a difference," answered the fox.

Next came the dinner to celebrate the coming wedding. So many courses of rich foods were served that the bewildered miller did not know which ones to take, nor indeed how to eat them.

"Why does your master not eat, brother fox?" asked the king. "Isn't he hungry?"

"How can he eat, Your Majesty? He is thinking of the thieves who robbed him on the road. You cannot imagine how much they took, nor what a blow the attack was to my master's dignity. How can he eat?" replied the fox.

"Ah-h-h, try not to worry, my dear son-in-law," consoled the king. "Such things happen. Let us hope future tragedies will be as small as this one. In the meantime, there is the wedding . . . Let us be merry and gay and forget sad things."

And so the wedding took place. For seven days and seven nights there was feasting and dancing and merriment.

The fox acted as the best man. The king presented his daughter a fine dowry, and after the seventh day he bade her farewell as she prepared to leave with her husband. According to the custom, the wedding guests formed a procession in order to escort the bride and groom to their own home.

"Do not hurry," said the fox to the guests. "Let me go on ahead and prepare the house a little to receive the bride." And he hurried on before them.

Soon he came upon a hillside of vast fields where herds of cattle were grazing.

"Who owns these herds of cattle?" the fox questioned the nearby farmers.

"Why, the shah, of course," they replied.

"Bah! Never speak of the shah again—or it will go ill with you. The king who follows right behind me with his guards is very angry with the shah and orders anyone beheaded who mentions his name. If he should ask you who owns these herds, answer, 'The miller-king,' or your heads will suffer!"

With this warning, the fox hurried on. Soon he came upon grazing flocks of sheep.

"Who owns these flocks of sheep?" asked the fox.

"Why, the shah, of course," replied the shepherds.

Repeating the same warning as before, the fox hurried on. He came to vast acres of farmland being tilled by hard-working farmers.

"Who owns these farmlands?" he asked.

"Why, the shah, of course," was the answer.

The fox repeated his warning.

He came upon hayfields where men were gathering hay.

"Who owns these hayfields?" the fox asked, and received the same answer: "Why, the shah, of course."

Once again, the fox repeated his warning. Finally, he reached a beautiful palace which was the residence of the shah himself.

"O shah, most honorable shah," said the fox, "do you see the cloud of dust in the road yonder? It is the king who comes with his soldiers. How can you sit so calmly? The king is angry with you and comes to kill you and take over all your possessions. Flee now—while there is yet time! Once I enjoyed your hospitality here, and since I never forget a kindness, I have come to warn you."

"What shall I do? Where shall I go?" cried the frightened shah, who could already see the king and his company far off in the distance.

"Go anywhere—as far from here as possible. Flee for your life," urged the fox, and he helped the shah escape from the back door of the palace.

In the meantime, the wedding procession continued down the road. It was led by the miller and his bride dressed in their royal garments and followed by the wedding guests and the horse guards walking to the music of the royal musicians.

The procession reached the herds of cattle.

"Who owns these herds?" asked the wedding guests.

"Why, the miller-king, of course," replied the farmers.

The procession reached the hillside where the flocks of sheep grazed peacefully.

"Who owns these sheep?" came the question.

"Why, the miller-king, of course," was the answer.

The procession continued on its way and came to the fields where the workers toiled.

"Who owns these fields?"

"Why, the miller-king, of course."

The procession reached the hayfields.

"Who owns these fields?" "Why, the miller-king, of course," replied the farmers.

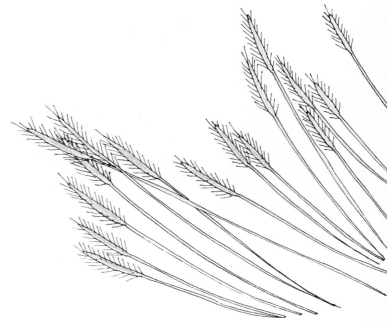

Amazed were all the wedding guests and soldier guards, but most amazed of all was the poor miller-bridegroom!

In this way, the procession finally reached the front gate of the shah's palace where the fox, the best man, welcomed the bride and groom and their guests. Once again the feasting and merrymaking started, and continued for seven days and seven nights until the guests and soldier guards finally bid the bridal couple farewell and left for home.

The miller-king and his bride lived happily in their palace, and with them lived happily ever after the fox. As for the shah—no one has ever heard of him since that time. Probably he is running away from the angry miller-king to this very day.

The Master and the Servant

ONCE THERE WAS AND WAS NOT IN ANCIENT ARMENIA a pair of brothers so poor they could not keep a roof over their heads. They finally decided that while the younger brother remained at home to tend house, the elder would go out to look for work that would support them both.

After some searching, the elder brother at last found employment as the servant of a very rich man.

"If you agree to work for me, however," said the rich man, "you must promise to stay until the call of the cuckoo in the spring."

The elder brother agreed.

"There is still another condition," the rich man went on. "You must agree to a bargain. You must promise not to lose your temper while you are working for me. If you should lose it, you must pay me one thousand silver pieces as forfeit. On the other hand, if I lose my temper, I'll pay you one thousand silver pieces. What do you say? Do you agree to the bargain?"

"But I don't own one thousand silver pieces," protested the elder brother.

"In that case, instead of paying the money, you must work for me for ten years," said the rich man.

At first, the elder brother was afraid to agree to such a bargain. "But I really have no choice," he thought to himself. "My brother and I need the money and I will just make up my mind not to lose my temper no matter what my master does."

"It's a bargain!" he said aloud.

Both master and servant signed an agreement, and the elder brother started to work.

Early the next morning, the rich master sent the servant out to the fields to harvest the grain.

"Go quickly," he ordered, "and continue working while it's light. Come back only when darkness falls."

The servant hurried to the fields. He worked hard all that day and when twilight came he returned home, tired and weary.

"Why have you come back so soon?" asked the rich man.

"The sun has set—and so I came home."

"That's not what I told you to do!" shouted the master angrily. "I told you to work while there was light. It is true that the sun has set, but the moon has come out. That gives light!"

"What kind of reasoning is that?" exclaimed the amazed elder brother.

"What! Are you losing your temper?" asked the master.

"No! I'm not losing my temper," stammered the elder brother. "What I meant to say was that I'm a little tired and I ought to rest."

Wearily, the elder brother returned to the fields. He worked hard and long by moonlight. Then as soon as the moon disappeared, the sun rose from the east. He continued to work by sunlight until, exhausted, he fell to the ground.

"To the devil with your farm and your money and with you, too!" murmured the youth wearily.

"What! Have you lost your temper?" asked the master, suddenly appearing in the fields. "Remember our bargain!

If you have lost your temper, you must either give me one thousand silver pieces or ten years of your service."

The poor youth did not know what to do. He neither had one thousand pieces of silver—nor could he bear to work for such a taskmaster for ten long years. In despair, he gave the master a signed note, promising to pay him one thousand silver pieces in the future. Then, empty-handed, he returned home to his brother.

"Did you make a fortune?" the younger brother greeted the elder. And the elder brother told him everything that had happened.

"Stay home and rest yourself. Don't worry," said the younger brother consolingly. "It's my turn to find work while you tend house." And he went immediately to the home of the same rich man to ask for work as a servant.

"If you want to work for me," said the rich man, "you must promise to stay until the call of the cuckoo in the spring."

The younger brother agreed. The rich master offered the same bargain to the younger brother: If the boy should lose his temper, he must forfeit one thousand silver pieces or ten years of service as a servant. If the master should lose his temper first, however, he must forfeit one thousand silver pieces.

"Is it a bargain?" asked the rich man.

"Oh, no! That's hardly worth bargaining for," scoffed the younger brother. "If you lose your temper, you must pay me two thousand pieces of silver. If I lose my temper, I will either forfeit two thousand silver pieces or work for you for twenty years."

"It's a bargain!" The greedy master quickly agreed to the new terms. They signed the agreement, and the younger brother started to work.

Night passed and morning came, but the young servant did not get out of bed. The master angrily paced the floor; the servant still slept. Finally, the master rushed into the boy's bedroom. "Get up! Get up! Do you realize it's nearly noon?" he shouted.

"What! Are you by chance losing your temper?" asked the servant, lifting his head from the pillow.

33

"Of course I'm not losing my temper!" answered the frightened master, lowering his voice. "I'm only reminding you that we must go to harvest the grain."

"Oh, well, then . . . if you're not angry, we'll go right along," said the boy. Slowly he got out of bed and slowly began to put on his clothes.

The rich man impatiently paced back and forth—and still the boy continued to dress.

"Hurry, boy! You're taking too long to get dressed!" exclaimed the master.

"What! Are you losing your temper?" asked the servant.

"Who is losing his temper? Certainly not I! I just mean to remind you that we are late!"

"Oh, well, then . . . I will be ready soon," replied the younger brother.

By the time the servant finished dressing, by the time they arrived at the fields, it was already noon.

"It would look silly to start work now when all the others are eating their noon meal," said the servant. "Let's eat first; then we can go to work."

They sat down together and ate. "It is customary for working people to take a short nap after a noonday meal," said the younger brother and stretched himself out on the ground. He fell asleep at once and did not wake up till nightfall.

"Wake up! Wake up! It's dark already and only our grain is not yet harvested. Cursed be the one who sent you to me! I'm ruined!" shouted the rich man in despair.

"What! Can it be you are losing your temper?" asked the servant, waking up.

"Who's losing his temper? I'm not!" the master exclaimed. "I only mean to remind you that night has fallen. It's time to go home."

"Oh, well, then . . . that's different. I thought you might have forgotten our bargain."

They returned to the house to find that unexpected guests had arrived. The master ordered the servant to go out and kill a sheep for supper.

"Which one?" asked the boy.

"Whichever one comes along," answered the master impatiently. "But hurry!"

A few moments later, some of the other servants came running in to their master.

"Master! Master! Hurry! Your new servant has killed all the sheep in your flock!"

The rich man rushed out and found that all his sheep had, indeed, been slaughtered. Out of his mind with anger, he shouted to the boy, "What have you done, you fool? May your house be ruined as you have ruined mine! Why have you killed all my sheep?"

"But master, you told me to kill whichever sheep came along. They all came along—and I killed them all according to your orders. And I do think you've lost your temper this time, haven't you?"

"No! I have NOT lost my temper," screamed the master. "Alas! I am only heartbroken to have lost all my sheep."

"Oh, well, then . . . as long as you haven't lost your temper, I'll continue to work for you," replied the servant.

From that moment on, however, the rich man thought only of how he could get rid of his servant. By their agreement, the boy was to work until the call of the cuckoo in the spring. It was still winter, however, and the spring cuckoo was months away.

Finally, the master thought of a plan. He took his wife into the woods, put her up in a tree, and told her to call, *Cuckoo, cuckoo* when he returned later with the servant.

Back at the house, he ordered the servant to accompany him on a hunting trip into the woods. As soon as the two entered the woods, the man's wife in the tree called out, *Cuckoo, cuckoo!*

"Aha!" said the master. "Listen! There is the call of the cuckoo, I do believe. According to our agreement, your months of work for me are over."

The younger brother thought for a moment. He suspected a plot.

"No! No! Who ever heard of a cuckoo singing in the middle of winter? It must be a very strange cuckoo, indeed. I will kill it immediately." Saying this, he aimed his bow at the tree.

The rich man fell upon the younger brother. "Don't shoot! Don't shoot! Ah-h-h-h—black was the day you came to me!" he shouted. "What trouble I'm in because of you!"

"What! Is it possible you are losing your temper?" asked the servant.

"Yes! Yes! Yes! I'm losing my temper! This is enough! I'll pay any price to get rid of you! I made the bargain—and I'll suffer the losses! Just get out of my sight!" screamed the rich man at the top of his voice.

So it was that the rich man eagerly paid two thousand silver pieces to the servant. The younger brother, in turn, paid off his elder brother's debt of one thousand silver pieces. Then he put the remaining one thousand silver pieces into his pocket and headed happily for home.

The Talking Fish

ONCE THERE WAS AND WAS NOT IN ANCIENT ARMENIA
a man who was very poor—and though he tried to better
himself, still he remained poor. At last he was able to find
work as a fisherman's helper. Thus he could bring home a fish
or two each day, which enabled him and his wife to live.

One day the fisherman caught an unusually beautiful
fish, which he handed to his helper to put into the fish sack.
It was still early so the fisherman then went off to fish some
more.

The fisherman's helper gazed long and thoughtfully at the fish in his hands. "Oh, Lord," he thought, "this is a breathing living creature, like us. Tell me, does this fish not have parents as we do? And friends? Doesn't he, too, understand something of this world? Doesn't he feel happiness and pleasure and pain as we do?"

As the man silently thought these things, the fish began to speak in a human voice.

"Listen to me, brother man," he said. "I was playing in the river rapids. In my pleasure, I forgot to be careful and fell into the fisherman's net. And now—now, I know that my parents are searching for me, and weeping at my absence. My friends are saddened, and I, as you can see for yourself, am panting for breath and fighting for my very life.

"I want to return to my family, to play in the clear water once again. Ah, fisherman's helper, take pity on me. Throw me back into the river. Give me my freedom. Open the net and let me go."

Thus pleaded the fish in a faint voice while his mouth opened and closed in weaker and weaker gasps.

The fisherman's helper took pity on the fish. He lifted him up and threw him back into the river.

"Go, sweet fish," he said, "your parents must not weep, nor should your friends be saddened. Go to live and play among them."

When the fisherman returned to find that his helper had released the fish, he was furious and scolded the man sharply. "You fool!" he shouted. "I work hard catching fish, and you take the result of my labor to throw it back into the river! Go and die from starvation for all I care!" Seizing the empty sack from his helper's hands, he pushed him on his way.

"Ah-h-h, now where shall I go? What shall I do? How shall we live?" despaired the poor man as he made his way homeward to his wife.

It happened that along the way he met a demon leading a cow behind him. Although the demon was in the disguise of a human being, the man recognized him nevertheless.

"Good day, brother-to-be," called out the demon. "Why do you look so grieved? What painful thoughts make you look so sad?"

The poor man recounted all that had happened to him and how he was now out of work with no hope of employment and no means of livelihood for himself and his wife.

"Listen to me, friend," said the demon. "I will make a bargain with you. I will lend you this milk cow. You may keep her for exactly three years and each day she will give enough milk for you and your wife to live more than comfortably.

"At the end of that time, however, I shall come and ask you a question. If you answer correctly, my cow is yours. 43

Otherwise, you and your wife belong to me and must do my bidding forever. Is it a bargain? What do you say?"

The poor man thought quickly. "One thing is certain," he said to himself. "Without the cow, we shall starve. With the cow, at least we shall live comfortably for three years. And who knows what will happen then? God is good—and a door to good luck may open somehow. We might even be able to think of the right answer to the demon's question. Who knows?"

"It is a bargain," agreed the poor man and, leading the cow, he made for home.

For three years, the man and his wife milked the cow, and the sale of leftover milk, cream, butter and cheese brought them the extras of life. Indeed, they were so happy that they did not heed the swift passing of time until the three years were up and the day of the demon's visit was at hand.

45

The man and his wife did their daily chores with heavy hearts, and at dusk sat sadly in front of the house wondering how they were to answer the fateful question to be put to them. Who could tell what the demon would ask? What human being could read the mind of a demon? Alas! Anything might happen when a man did business with a demon, or accepted favors from one!

Too late, the man regretted the bargain he had made three years ago, although at that time, he told himself, he had had no other choice.

As dusk deepened into night, and the couple anxiously awaited the demon's coming, a handsome young stranger approached them.

"Good evening," he said. "I have traveled a long way. It is very late and I am tired. Would you accept a guest this night?"

"Why not, brother traveler? A guest belongs to God and man. But we must warn you that is it dangerous to be near us tonight. Three years ago we borrowed a cow belonging to a demon on condition that he be permitted to ask us a question at the end of that time. If we answer correctly, the cow is ours. Otherwise, we become his slaves. Now the time is up; the demon is to come this very night and we don't know how to answer him. Whatever happens, we are to blame, but what if harm comes to you, young stranger?"

"Don't worry about me," smiled the strange youth. "Whatever happens, I shall share your fate."

In the middle of the night after all three had wearily retired there came a loud knock at the door.

"Who is it?" called the man.

"The demon. I have come; I want my answer."

"What answer?" The couple were so frightened they could hardly speak.

"Don't be frightened," said the strange youth. "I shall answer him in your place. Do not say another word."

"I've come," repeated the demon.

"I have come, also," replied the stranger from behind the door.

"Where have you come from?" the demon demanded.

"From the far shores of the sea."

"How did you get here?"

"I saddled the lame water buffalo and mounted it to come," replied the stranger.

"Was the sea so narrow, then, that you could cross it thus?"

"Narrow! Why, the sea is so vast that an eagle cannot fly from one shore to another."

"Is an eagle so tiny, then?"

"Tiny! Why, the shadow of an eagle's wings can cover a whole city!"

"Well then, is a city so small?"

"Small! Even a swift hare cannot run from one end to the other without weariness."

"Well then, is a hare so little?"

"Little! Why, its fur will stretch to make a grown man's coat—and his hat and boots besides!"

"Well then, is a man such a dwarf?"

"A dwarf! Why, a rooster crowing from a man's knee can hardly be heard by the man's ear."

"Well then, is a man deaf?"

"Deaf! Why, a man can hear the sound of an insect eating grain in the field."

The demon was thoroughly confused by now; he realized that behind the door stood a wise and unbeatable spirit. Knowing that he was beaten, the evil one disappeared silently into the darkness.

The old couple, saved from an unknown fate, rejoiced at their good fortune, and finally all three returned to bed. In the morning, the young traveler thanked the couple for their hospitality and prepared to depart.

"We cannot let you go. You have saved our lives," exclaimed the old man and his wife. "How can we ever repay your kindness? You must stay longer with us."

48

The stranger insisted that he must leave and said he expected no payment.

"At least, tell us your name," begged the old couple. "If we can't repay you, at least we will know whom to bless in our prayers."

"A kindness is never lost—even if it is thrown into the water," said the stranger. "I am the talking fish whose life you saved three years ago. And I came here to repay my debt."

With that, the young stranger disappeared before the eyes of the old man and his wife.

Shrovetide

(Carnival days of merrymaking just before Lent)

ONCE THERE WAS AND WAS NOT IN ANCIENT ARMENIA a couple who could not get along with one another. The man called his wife a fool; the wife called her husband the same—and they argued from morn till night.

One day the man went to the village and brought home one hundred measures of rice and fifty measures of butter. When the wife saw so much rice and butter, she lost her temper.

"When I call you a fool, you get angry," she shouted, "but fool you are! Why did you buy so much rice and butter? Are you going to celebrate your son's wedding or your father's name day?"

"What wedding! What name day! Stop shouting!" answered the husband. "I bought this for Shrovetide."

The wife quieted down and put away the rice and butter.

Several weeks passed. The wife waited and waited patiently but Shrovetide did not come. One day while she sat alone outside her front door, she saw a stranger walking down the street with quick determined steps.

"Oh brother, brother," she called to him. "Stop a moment."

The man stopped.

"Brother, tell me. Are you, by chance, Shrovetide?"

The stranger realized that the woman was not quite right in her head and, in order to humor her, he replied, "Yes, sister, I am, indeed, Shrovetide. What do you want of me?"

"Well, I want to say that I think it's about time you appeared! We are not your servants, you know! We have kept your rice and butter long enough! Come and take them away at once!"

"Don't be angry, my sister," answered the man, smiling.

"I was just coming to get my rice and butter, but I couldn't seem to find the right house!"

"Well, now that you have found it, take away your property." The stranger walked into the house, took the one hundred measures of rice and the fifty measures of butter and left.

Soon afterwards, the woman's husband returned home.

"Well," said the wife, "Shrovetide finally came and I gave him his things!"

"What Shrovetide? What things?"

"Why, the rice and butter, of course. I saw him walking towards our house searching for us. I hailed him, scolded him properly and gave him his things."

"Oh, you fool! I always said you were a fool! Which way did he go?" shouted the angry husband.

"That way."

Jumping on his horse, the husband went in search of Shrovetide. Further along the road the stranger heard someone following him. He turned around, and guessed that the rider must be the husband of the foolish woman. Quickly he hid the rice and butter behind some bushes.

"Good day, brother," the husband greeted the stranger.

"Good day to you."

"Have you seen anyone else traveling along this road?"

"Why yes, I have."

"Did he, by chance, carry a large bundle on his back?"

"Yes, he had some rice and butter."

"Ah, that's the man I seek," said the husband. "How long ago did he pass?"

"Oh, quite some time ago."

"Will I catch up to him if my horse hurries?"

"I don't think so," answered the stranger. "Your horse would have to hurry along on his four feet, while the man could hurry along on his two feet much faster, since he has less feet to worry about."

"Then what shall I do?" asked the foolish husband.

"Well, why don't you leave your horse with me? With only your own two feet to worry about, you could probably overtake him," answered the crafty stranger.

"You speak the truth; if you would be kind enough to mind my horse, I'll do as you say." And the foolish husband dismounted. Leaving his horse with the stranger, he hurried along on foot.

As soon as he disappeared down the road, Shrovetide loaded the rice and butter on the back of the horse and rode off in the opposite direction.

Meanwhile, the husband walked and walked and overtook no one. In disgust, he returned to the place where he had left his horse and found neither horse nor stranger. Wearily, he went home and told his wife all that had happened.

Once again they began to argue. He called her a fool and shouted about the rice and butter. She called him a bigger fool and screamed about the horse. They argued from morn till night, and no doubt are arguing till this very day.

As for Shrovetide: he probably hears them and smiles. 55

The White Snake

ONCE THERE WAS AND WAS NOT IN ANCIENT ARMENIA a very wise king who seemed to have knowledge of all things. It was as though the wind whispered the most secret of secrets into his ear.

Every day, the king practiced a most peculiar custom. Before each meal, a certain servant was ordered to bring a small covered dish to the royal bedroom, place it on the table, and then depart—leaving the king alone with the dish.

This peculiar custom continued for some years, until one day the servant could no longer contain his curiosity. Before bringing the dish to the king, he first carried it secretly into his own room—and slowly uncovered it . . . A cooked white snake lay coiled within the dish.

Unable to stop himself, the servant cut off a piece of the snake meat and ate it. As soon as his tongue touched the meat, the youth was aware of a peculiar chirping and warbling of birds on the branches of the trees just outside the open window of his room.

He listened, and to his astonishment, realized that he was able to understand the language of the birds! And as he heard the many tales told to each other by the birds and insects on the trees, the servant knew that the snake meat which he had swallowed had given him the power to understand the speech of all animals.

It so happened that on that very day, the queen lost her most prized ring. Since this faithful servant was the only one who had access to all rooms in the palace, suspicion fell upon him—and the courtiers declared that he must, indeed be the thief!

The king summoned the youth and threatened him: "If the ring is not returned by sunrise tomorrow, OFF WITH YOUR HEAD!"

The servant swore his innocence, but the king would not listen. "You will produce either the ring or the identity of the thief by sunrise tomorrow if you wish to keep your head," he repeated.

Trembling with fear and anger, the faithful servant went out to the courtyard to think of a way out of his predicament. As he paced back and forth, his eyes absently gazed upon some ducks in the nearby pond. They were huddled together, resting and cleaning their feathers with their flat bills. They were probably telling each other of the tasty catch of fish which each had had for breakfast that morning.

One of them stretched up and boasted, "As for me, I admit I was too greedy! I swallowed the queen's ring that had fallen beneath her window. But I'm paying for it, now! My stomach feels so heavy and tight!"

The servant leaped forward and grabbed the duck by his neck. He ran to the kitchen with the squawking bird and shouted to the cook, "Kill and pluck this duck! He has grown too fat for his own good!"

"You are right," agreed the cook. "He is a fat one, indeed—just right for roasting." And with that, he chopped off the duck's head. As he cleaned the bird's stomach, out came the queen's ring.

Thus, the servant was cleared of blame. The king, ashamed of his doubt of the boy, offered to grant him any request he wished to make, as well as a permanent place in the palace.

The servant refused all favors. He begged only for the gift of a horse, enough money for a few meals, and his freedom to go out and see the world. And with the king's blessing, he set off.

He traveled far; he traveled wide. One day he came upon three fish lying by the side of a brook. They had accidentally leaped out of the water, and now, unable to get back in, they lay helpless, dying of thirst.

The servant listened to the fish telling one another of their sad fate. He felt sorry for them and, dismounting from his horse, threw them back into the brook. At first, the half-dead fish swam in circles under the surface of the water, trying to revive themselves. Then they raised their heads out of the brook and called out, "We will never forget your kindness to us, good lad. Some day, perhaps, we shall be able to reward you."

The servant continued on his way. Soon he became aware of a faint moaning sound beneath his feet. He looked down and saw a swarm of crawling ants. He bent an ear down to the ground and heard the ants complaining. "Alas! If only big men and giant beasts would leave us alone—and walk elsewhere! See how this stupid horse with his enormous feet tramples our homes and families."

The servant felt sorry for the ants and turned his horse off to a side path, whereupon the king of the ants hailed the youth. "Thanks, kind soul. With God's help, we will not be long beholden to you."

The youth traveled up the narrow path into the forest. As he passed under a tree, he heard two crows fluttering about on the edge of their nest and soundly scolding their young.

"Children, we can't find food for you forever! You're

old enough now to go seek your own food. Get up and fly!"

The frightened, hungry young crows tried to test their wings, but fell to the ground, cawing wildly.

We're baby crows—unwanted and poor.
We have no nest, nor wings that are sure.
Where shall we find food and a home, too?
Where shall we go—what shall we do?

The servant's heart was filled with pity. Without thinking of the long or the short of it, he gave the baby crows the few crumbs of bread he had left from his last meal.

"Thank you, lad," called the crows. "Be sure we will repay your kindness some day."

The youth continued on his way and traveled far until he reached a large city where the streets were filled with excited people. Soon a royal messenger on horseback came down the street, calling out to all who would listen:

"THE KING'S DAUGHTER SEEKS A HUSBAND. WHOSOEVER WISHES THE POSITION MUST PERFORM A HEROIC DEED. IF SUCCESSFUL, HE GAINS THE PRINCESS AS WIFE; IF HE FAILS, HE SHALL FORFEIT HIS HEAD."

In the next few days, many brave young men came to try for the position—and lost their heads for their trouble.

One day, however, the servant saw the king's daughter at the palace window. Immediately he fell deeply in love with her. Though he knew the dangers and pitfalls connected with the venture, he presented himself at the palace and asked for the hand of the princess.

He was accepted as a candidate and escorted immediately to the shore of the sea. There the king himself took a gold ring from his finger, threw it into the sea and said, "This shall be your heroic deed. You must retrieve my ring from the sea. If you succeed, my daughter is yours. If you fail, you shall yourself be thrown into the sea to drown."

The courtiers who accompanied the king, and the common people besides, felt sorry for the brave youth who was about to drown. But while he pondered his fate for a moment, three fish came swimming toward the servant—the same fish he had rescued in the past. The middle one carried a seashell in his mouth, which he dropped in front of the waiting youth. When the lad picked it up, he found the gold ring resting inside.

The rejoicing of the servant and the courtiers was quickly cut short when the proud princess scorned the humble servant for her husband. She demanded further proof of his worth and imposed a second test.

The princess went into the fields behind the palace and

with her own hands gathered ten bags of grain. She then scattered the grain upon the ground. "You must gather every bit of this grain into the ten bags before sunrise," she said. "If you miss even one kernel, you will lose your head."

Left alone in the field, the poor servant once again pondered his miserable fate and, being weary, fell asleep. When he awakened in the morning, he could hardly believe his eyes. There, resting before him, were ten bags of grain neatly packed—and nary a kernel on the ground! The ants whom he had befriended in the past had returned his favor and collected the grain.

Although the king's daughter received the grain with amazement, she was still not ready to accept the humble youth as husband.

"You have successfully performed two tasks," she said, "but in order to become my husband, you must bring me the sacred apple from the Tree of Life."

The youth had never heard of such an apple, nor did he know where it might be found. Nevertheless, he started on his way, traveling from mountain to valley in search of the sacred apple.

One day, tired and discouraged, he sat beneath a tree in a forest to rest. Suddenly he heard a rustling of leaves above him—and a golden apple dropped into his lap. Then three crows flew down from the top of the tree and alighted on the servant's knee.

"We are the three crows whom you once saved from starvation. When we grew up and heard of your search for the sacred apple from the Tree of Life, we traveled over hill and ocean to bring you the apple you seek."

The servant thanked the crows, and with the sacred apple in his hand, started on his way back to the princess.

The princess gazed upon the fruit. "I have no further objection to you as my husband," she said to the youth, whereupon they halved the apple and ate it together. Immediately, the princess's heart was filled with love for the servant.

They were married—and lived happily ever after.

Nazar the Brave

ONCE THERE WAS AND WAS NOT IN ANCIENT ARMENIA a peasant named Nazar who was both lazy and stupid. Worse than that, Nazar was a terrible coward. He was afraid of everything: of the light and of the dark, of the day and of the night. He did not dare to take a step by himself. Hanging on to his wife's apron strings from morning till night, he followed the poor woman wherever she went.

Thus people called him Nazar the Fearful.

One night his wife stepped out to the back of the house for a moment. As usual Nazar followed right behind her. It was a brilliant, moonlit night and the stars shone brightly over the mountains.

"Ah, wife," sighed Nazar, "what a wonderful night for a robbery! My heart tells me to go and rob the caravan of the rich shah who visits our land from India."

"Oh, be still!" said his wife angrily. "Who are you to talk of robbing a caravan!"

"Why won't you let me rob the shah's caravan?" scolded Nazar. "That's just the way you are! Never letting me do anything! Am I not a man? Do I not wear the hat of a man? Why do you stop me?"

Sick of her husband's empty boasts, Nazar's wife ran into the house and slammed the door in his face.

"All right," she called out. "Go ahead and rob the shah's caravan. And don't come back here till you do!"

Poor Nazar was frightened out of his wits at this turn of events. In vain did he beg and plead with his wife to rescue him.

The hours passed. Weariness finally overcame him and he fell asleep.

The night was a hot and sticky one, and morning came
slowly. Thousands of flies swarmed over Nazar's face, stick-
ing to his nose and his lips. Without opening his eyes, and
still half asleep, he angrily raised his hand and slapped at the
flies. Dead flies fell all about him. Nazar opened his eyes and
saw the dead flies on the ground beside him.

"What is this?" he said in amazement. And he began   73

to count the number of flies he had killed at one blow. There were so many that he lost count.

"Ah! What a brave man I am! And I never knew it until today! To think that I who can kill a thousand living things at one blow have been waiting hand and foot on such an ungrateful wife as mine!"

Quickly he got up and went off to see the village priest. "Bless me, Father," he said.

"God's blessings on you, my son," replied the priest.

"Father, you don't know . . . let me tell you . . ." And Nazar recounted the tale of his bravery. He begged the priest to record his courageous deed so that all might know of it.

Laughing, the good-natured priest took a piece of cloth and, in jest, printed in large letters the words:

NAZAR THE BRAVE, OUR MIGHTY HERO,

FELLS A THOUSAND AT A SINGLE BLOW.

Nazar attached the cloth to the end of a long pole as a banner, tucked a rusty sword he had found into his belt, mounted his neighbor's donkey and rode off. He traveled and traveled on a road which led out of the village and through a forest.

As he left his home farther and farther behind, Nazar became more and more frightened. To keep up his spirits, he began to talk to himself and to scold the poor donkey in loud tones. The farther he traveled, the more frightened he became, and the more frightened he was, the louder he shouted. The poor bewildered donkey brayed louder in reply.

All this commotion disturbed the peace of the birds, who started to screech. The timid rabbits scurried into their burrows, and the frogs jumped into the water from their lily pads.

A well-to-do peasant, who was leading his horse back from market through the forest, heard all the noise and shouting.

"Oh my!" said the peasant. "It must be thieves!" Leaving his horse in the forest, he took to his heels and fled for his life.

When Nazar approached the spot, he saw a horse with an expensive saddle standing unattended. Getting off his donkey, he mounted the horse and continued on his way.

He traveled and traveled . . . how far he did not know, until he reached a village from which came sounds of the zoorna.* A wedding feast was in progress in the center of the village.

"Good day," said Nazar as he rode toward the gathered wedding guests and dismounted.

"Good day to you, stranger, and a thousand welcomes. Come and join us. Any guest is both God's and ours."

*Bugle.

The villagers took Nazar with his banner, to the head of the table and offered him food and drink. They were curious to know who this stranger might be and what his banner said, but since they were simple peasants who could not read, the printed words remained a mystery. Each guest in turn nudged his neighbor and whispered, "Who is he?" until, finally, the question reached the village priest sitting at the head of the table.

The priest leaned over and spelled out the words on the banner:

NAZAR THE BRAVE, OUR MIGHTY HERO,
FELLS A THOUSAND AT A SINGLE BLOW.

He read them to himself, repeated them to the one sitting next to him, who, in turn, repeated it to his neighbor—all the way down to the foot of the table until all the wedding guests knew the identity of the guest.

NAZAR THE BRAVE, OUR MIGHTY HERO,
FELLS A THOUSAND AT A SINGLE BLOW.

"Ah-h-h," said one who loved to boast. "So it's Nazar the Brave! Oh, I remember him well, but I didn't recognize him. He has changed greatly since I saw him last."

Several others pretended to remember him and began to whisper to one another what they remembered of Nazar's past bravery.

"But if he is so famous and important, how is it that he has no servant to attend him?" asked one of the guests.

"That is his desire," replied another. "He is too humble to keep a servant. Once I, too, asked him that very question and he answered that the whole world was his servant. What need did he have for one?"

"But how is it that such a man carries no real sword—only a small rusty one in his belt?" another guest wondered aloud.

"What need would Nazar have for a large shiny blade? Anyone can be brave with a sharp weapon. Only Nazar can perform bravely with a small rusty one!" came the reply.

The astonished villagers were very impressed with the famous guest. They drank many toasts in his honor. The village orator arose and with great dignity delivered a long speech of welcome to the hero, while the village troubador sang a song praising his deeds of valor.

When darkness finally ended the wedding celebration, the villagers presented Nazar with gifts and bade him farewell.

Nazar rode away from the village, trembling with fear at the darkness and the strange unfamiliar roads. Finally he reached a wide, open green field. Frightened and weary, he dismounted to let his horse graze. He thrust his banner into the ground, huddled fearfully beneath it and fell asleep.

The field belonged to seven giants, who lived in a castle on top of the mountain overlooking the open space. In the morning the giants looked out and saw that someone had dared trespass on their land. Angrily, they shouldered their clubs and tramped down to the field to find Nazar fast asleep under a banner which read:

NAZAR THE BRAVE, OUR MIGHTY HERO,

FELLS A THOUSAND AT A SINGLE BLOW.

"It's Nazar the Brave!" exclaimed the giants. "The hero we have heard so much about from all the villagers." And they gazed fearfully at the man who could kill a thousand at a single blow.

Suddenly Nazar awoke. When he opened his eyes and saw seven giants armed with clubs towering over him, his stomach turned over! Trembling like a fall leaf he tried to crawl under his banner.

When the giants saw him turn pale and tremble, they were frightened.

"Nazar the Brave is angry," they said. "And now he will kill us at one blow." They fell upon their knees before Nazar and pleaded with him.

"Oh, Nazar the Brave, we have heard of your fame and have long wished to meet you. We are honored to have you as our guest. Come to our home on top of yonder hill and meet our beautiful sister. Accept us as your servants and brothers and do us the honor of breaking bread with us."

Nazar collected his wits and permitted himself to be led to the giants' castle, where he was treated as an honored guest. Indeed, so well did the giants tell the tales of Nazar's bravery to their beautiful sister, Yar, that she promptly fell in love with him.

79

About this time, a man-eating tiger suddenly appeared in the countryside, terrifying the people. All agreed that the tiger must be killed—but who was brave enough to try? "Nazar the Brave, of course! Who else?" exclaimed the villagers, and they came to Nazar for help.

As soon as Nazar heard the word tiger, he began to shake with fright and ran out of the castle to go back to his own village and his wife.

The people, however, thought that he was running to kill the tiger.

The beautiful Yar called after him, "Nazar, my brave hero, where do you go without weapons? At least take this knife with you." And she hurriedly brought him a knife to help him perform his deed of bravery.

Grabbing the knife, Nazar ran into the forest as fast as he could go and scrambled to the top of the tallest tree he could find. Scared out of his wits, he held on for dear life, hoping never to see the tiger.

As luck would have it, the tiger chose that very moment to walk through the forest, and decided to lie down and rest under that same tree!

When Nazar looked down and saw the tiger, his liver turned to water. He trembled and shook so that he lost his hold on the tree. Down he fell, right on the back of the tiger!

The startled beast jumped up, furiously trying to shake off the strange burden on his back. Roaring wildly, the tiger ran out of the forest, while Nazar, quaking with fear, hung on for dear life.

What a sight it was for the people who waited on the outskirts of the village!

"Look!" they said. "Look! Nazar has tamed the tiger and is riding him like a horse!"

Gaining courage from Nazar's bravery, the villagers surrounded the tiger and killed him.

Slowly, Nazar regained his senses. Taking a deep breath, he opened his eyes and said, "Alas! Why did you kill the beast? I was going to keep him for a horse!"

News of this new deed of bravery spread throughout the countryside. All the people turned out to welcome Nazar and do him honor. The beautiful Yar decided to marry the hero, who had by now forgotten all about his first wife. A wedding was celebrated for seven days and seven nights and there were many toasts to praise the courage of the groom and the beauty of the bride.

Some weeks later, the giants received word that their neighbor king from the south was marching against them in battle. This same king had long been in love with Yar and reports of her marriage to Nazar had angered him into an open declaration of war.

The giants came to Nazar for help. Proclaiming him general in charge of their armies, they gave him full command.

At mention of the word war, Nazar quaked with fear, and started to run out of the castle back to his own village.

The people thought that Nazar was rushing to fight the enemy with his bare hands.

"Come back, brave Nazar," they begged. "How can you go into battle unarmed and on foot?" The beautiful Yar pleaded with her brothers to restrain her brave husband.

News of Nazar's great courage spread throughout the army and made the soldiers eager to follow such a commander. Indeed, Nazar's fame spread even to the enemy.

The soldiers helped Nazar mount a horse saddled especially for battle. Hundreds of men on horseback waited for his commands. Nazar's horse moved, and off went the army to battle.

Nazar's horse, sensing that his rider had no control, bolted straight ahead toward the enemy camp. Nazar's soldiers, thinking that their commander was leading a charge, galloped after him.

When the frightened Nazar realized that his horse was leading him right into the midst of the enemy, he decided to save himself by jumping off the horse into a tree along the way. He grabbed for a branch, but the tree was a dead one, and a great part of it broke off in his hand!

When the enemy saw the famed hero, Nazar, galloping toward them with a tree in his hand, they cried, "Run for your lives! Nazar the Brave is coming to kill us, and he's tearing up the trees by the roots as he comes!"

Many were killed in that terrible battle. Those who survived surrendered to Nazar and swore him full allegiance.

What pomp and ceremony ushered Nazar back to the giants' castle! He was proclaimed king of the land by the grateful people and given all manner of gifts and honors. The seven giants became his seven viziers and helped him to rule wisely and well forever after.

But whenever the talk turned to his bravery and his courage, Nazar always smiled mysteriously and said, "What bravery! What courage! My friends, it is LUCK that rules the world."